For Jean and Marcia, who taught us how to fly.

Text copyright © 2018 by Matthew Heroux

Illustrations copyright © 2018 by Wednesday Kirwan

Book design by Melissa Nelson Greenberg

Library of Congress Control Number Catologing-in-Publication information available.

ISBN: 978-1-944903-35-0

Printed in China.

10 9 8 7 6 5 4 3 2 1

Cameron Kids is an imprint of Cameron + Company

Cameron + Company

Petaluma, California

www.cameronbooks.com

OWL LOVE YOU

BY MATTHEW HEROUX
& WEDNESDAY KIRWAN

cameron kids

The sun is setting. Open your eyes.
No more sleeping, little one, wake up! Surprise!

Hoo'll catch me when I flutter and fall?

Owl catch you, my dear, tail feathers and all.

Hoo'll fly by my side and keep me in sight?

Owl fly with you, love, like a moth to the light.

Hoo'll make up a song and sing me a tune?

Owl serenade you by the light of the moon.

Hoo'll play hide-and-seek and peek-a-boo, too?

Owl count while you hide and try to find you.

Hoo'll show me how to be curious and clever?

Owl show you the ropes, kid, now and forever.

Hoo'll hang with me when my friends aren't around?

Owl hang with you when things feel upside down.

Hoo'll race with me to the edge of the sky!

Owl race quick as a bunny. Now see how I fly.

Hoo'll scratch my back in that hard-to-reach place?

Owl scratch that spot, then I'll kiss your sweet face.

Hoo'll dance with me in the firefly light?

Owl dance with you as we twirl through the night.

Hoo'll carry me home when I'm ready to rest?

Owl carry you home to our soft, cozy nest.

Hoo'll snuggle with me when the night is through?

Owl snuggle and whisper, "Owl always love you!"